A girl named Saffy,
Smart and bright,

Her brother Ri,
A wise knight,

And Luna, their pup, fluffy and white,
Sought an adventure of fun and light!

Join the adventures of Saffy, Ri and Luna as they travel on their ship *Safina* to visit a beautiful coastal town by the sea.

See how they care and protect the environment and the animals that live there, as well as having fun at the beach!

Find the pawprints through the book and discover exciting colouring activities you can complete.

For my darlings

ISBN: 9798392556748

First publication, May 2023

Luna's Pawsitive Adventures

SEASIDE STORY

This book belongs to:

....

Author: Sheilla Jamani

golden ray.

Upon the sun's first
Three friends set sail one fine day.

From land's afar, they came to see,
A wonderous coastal town by the sea.

They reached the quay, the morning aglow,
Where boats and fish swam to and fro.

Luna watched, her heart open wide,
With Saffy and Ri by her side.

With their hearts full of joy and delight
To the beach, they strode,

— so bright! —

Luna, Saffy and Ri, dug holes in the sand,

Chased seagulls as planned.

Building sandcastles and dreams,
With joyful smiles upon each face,
In the sand's warm embrace.

Luna, Saffy and Ri then joined a cause.

We need to keep clean,
The beach for the scene,
For marine life and people galore!

Soon the trio strolled along the golden sand,
To a lighthouse standing TALL on the strand.

From a distance, they observed with a glance,
Sea lions basking in the sun.

The trio discovered a realm of marine life,

Where dolphins,

Whales,

And porpoise wander,

Where octopus,

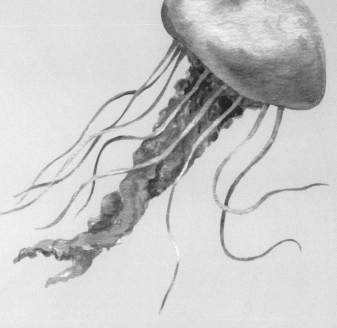

Jellyfish,

And starfish ponder.

Then came a sanctuary, where birds flew so free,
 A haven for creatures, a place to just be.

Luna learned the value of care,
Watching the birds high up in the air!

Soon they walked to the bustling market,
With Luna, who would not miss the target.

Wagging her tail, and sniffing sweet treats,
They found bric-a-brac in baskets.

They saw toys made of wood, without plastic,

Reuse and Recycle Ri said, enthusiastic,

For they cared for the earth,
And they knew the true worth,
Of keeping our oceans **fantastic!**

As the sun dipped low,
The sea's gentle flow,

Painted the skies aglow

With hearts full of love and devotion,
Saffy and Ri shared their emotion.

In Luna's heart, a promise she made
To protect the earth, her love displayed.

Reading Guidance Notes

Rhyming helps children learn about words, sounds and language formation, which is an essential early literacy skill.

The short rhymes provide bite-sized opportunities to learn about caring for the natural environment and the bio-diversity within it.

Read the rhymes in the story book with the child in a quiet space and encourage them to join in by repeating the rhymes.

The next few pages provide a mini colouring book that will help reinforce the characters, objects and places encountered in the book.

Printed in Great Britain
by Amazon

33477113R00021